## Nursery Rhymes

# Mary Had a Little Lamb

### and Other Best-loved Rhymes

alphabet
soup

an imprint of

WINDMILL
BOOKS
New York

Published in 2009 by Windmill Books, LLC
303 Park Avenue South, Suite # 1280, New York, NY 10010-3657

Illustrations by Ulkutay & Co. Ltd.
Editor: Rebecca Gerlings
Compiler: Paige Weber

      Publisher Cataloging Data

Mary had a little lamb and other best-loved rhymes / edited by Rebecca Gerlings.
p.      cm. – (Nursery rhymes)
Contents: Mary had a little lamb—Jack and Jill—Hot cross buns—
A tisket, a tasket—Cock-a-doodle-do!—What are little boys made of?
—Curly-locks—Baa, baa, black sheep—Here we go 'round the mulberry bush.
ISBN 978-1-60754-134-9 (library binding)
ISBN 978-1-60754-135-6 (paperback)
ISBN 978-1-60754-136-3 (6-pack)
1. Nursery rhymes  2. Children's poetry  [1. Nursery rhymes]
I. Gerlings, Rebecca  II. Mother Goose  III. Series
                   398.8—dc22

Printed in the United States

**For more great fiction and nonfiction, go to windmillbks.com.**

# CONTENTS

# Mary Had a Little Lamb

Mary had a little lamb,
Its fleece was white as snow,
And everywhere that Mary went,
The lamb was sure to go.

It followed her to school one day,
That was against the rule,
It made the children laugh and play,
To see a lamb at school.

So the teacher turned it out,
But still it lingered near,
And waited patiently about,
Till Mary did appear.

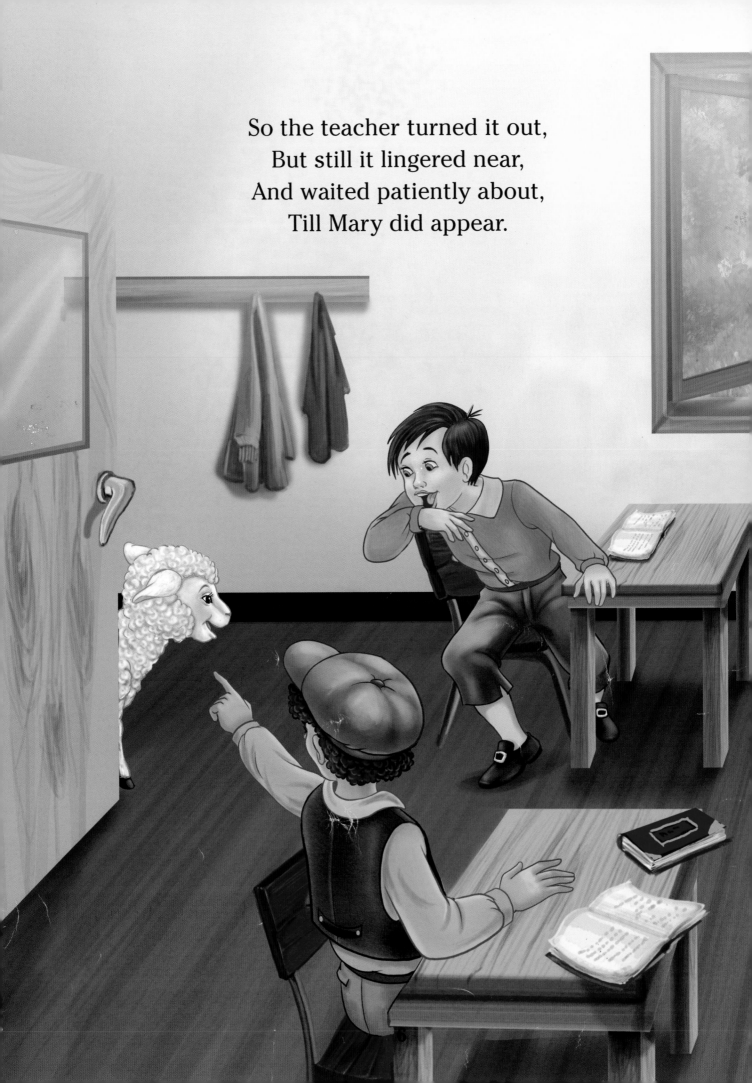

"What makes the lamb love Mary so?"
The eager children cry.
"Why, Mary loves the lamb, you know,"
The teacher did reply.

# Jack and Jill

Jack and Jill went up the hill,
To fetch a pail of water.
Jack fell down and broke his crown,
And Jill came tumbling after.

Then up Jack got, and home did trot,
As fast as he could caper,
Where his mother covered his head,
With vinegar and brown paper.

# Hot Cross Buns

Hot cross buns!
Hot cross buns!
One a penny, two a penny,
Hot cross buns!

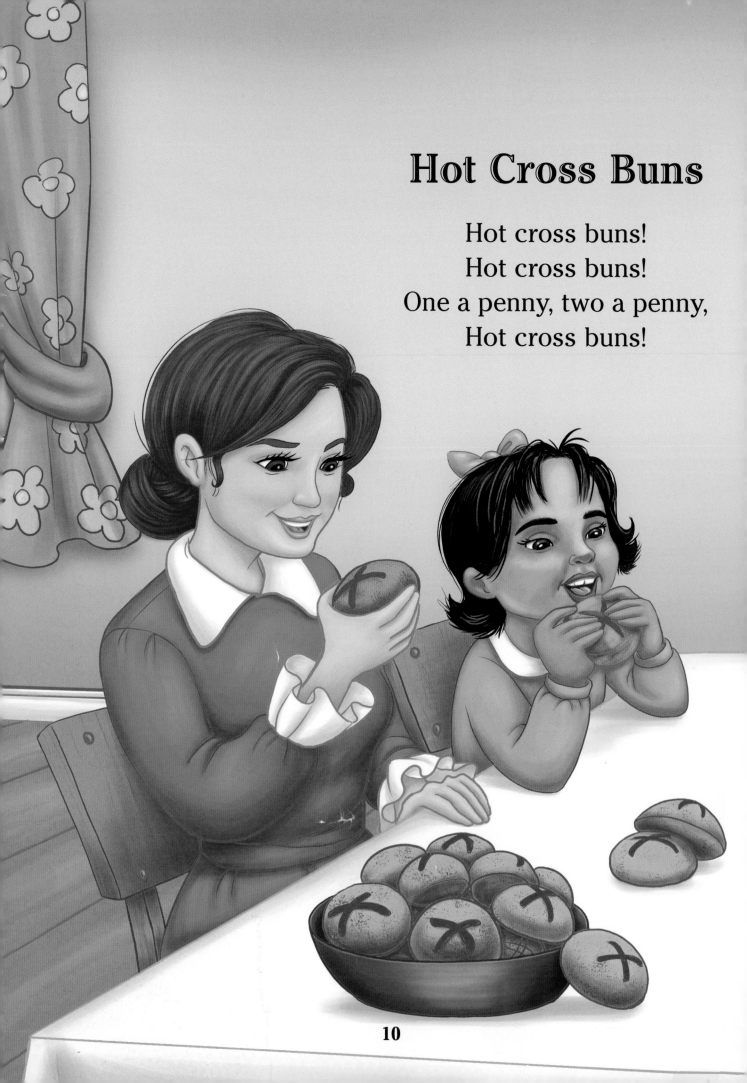

If you have no daughters,
Give them to your sons;
One a penny, two a penny,
Hot cross buns.

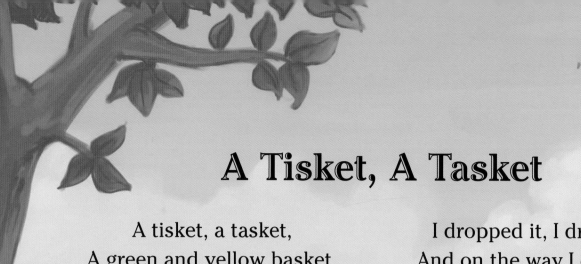

# A Tisket, A Tasket

A tisket, a tasket,
A green and yellow basket,
I wrote a letter to my love
And on the way I dropped it.

I dropped it, I dropped it,
And on the way I dropped it.
A little boy picked it up
And put it in his pocket.

# Cock-a-Doodle-Do!

Cock-a-doodle-do!
My dame has lost her shoe,
My master's lost his fiddlestick
And knows not what to do.

14

Cock-a-doodle-do!
What is my dame to do?
Till master finds his fiddlestick,
She'll dance without her shoe.

15

# What Are Little Boys Made of?

What are little boys made of?
What are little boys made of?
Snips and snails, and puppy dogs' tails;
That's what little boys are made of.

What are little girls made of?
What are little girls made of?
Sugar and spice, and all that's nice;
That's what little girls are made of.

# Curly-Locks

Curly-locks, curly-locks, wilt thou be mine?
Thou shalt not wash the dishes, nor yet feed the swine;
But sit on a cushion, and sew a fine seam,
And feed upon strawberries, sugar, and cream.

# Baa, Baa, Black Sheep

Baa, baa, black sheep,
Have you any wool?
Yes sir, yes sir,
Three bags full.

One for my master,
One for my dame,
And one for the little boy
Who lives down the lane.

Baa, baa, black sheep,
Have you any wool?
Yes sir, yes sir,
Three bags full.

21

# Here We Go 'Round the Mulberry Bush

Here we go 'round the mulberry bush,
The mulberry bush, the mulberry bush,
Here we go 'round the mulberry bush,
On a cold and frosty morning.

This is the way we wash our hands,
Wash our hands, wash our hands,
This is the way we wash our hands,
On a cold and frosty morning.

This is the way we wash our clothes,
Wash our clothes, wash our clothes,
This is the way we wash our clothes,
On a cold and frosty morning.

This is the way we go to school,
Go to school, go to school,
This is the way we go to school,
On a cold and frosty morning.

This is the way we come out of school,
Come out of school, come out of school,
This is the way we come out of school,
On a cold and frosty morning.

26

# ABOUT THE RHYMES

Nursery rhymes have been recited to children and by children for hundreds of years. They are an integral part of most people's childhoods, but where did these rhymes originate? Some nursery rhymes are more than just fun songs for adults and children to share with one another. In fact, the origins of many nursery rhymes in this book reflect events in history.

Their lyrics were often used as a way to mock royal and political events of the day in times when any direct challenge of the establishment could be punishable by death! It may seem strange that such events are still portrayed through children's nursery rhymes. Whether we realize their significance or not, nursery rhymes form a perpetual link between us and our past.

Because of the way spoken history is passed down, there are almost as many different interpretations of the rhymes' meanings as there are people who recite them, but the following are the most popular interpretations of some of the rhymes in this book. If your favorite isn't included here, see what you can find out yourself! They each have a special tale to tell.

# Mary Had a Little Lamb

Although many nursery rhymes originate from England, "Mary Had a Little Lamb" originates from North America. The rhyme is believed to be based upon the life of Mary Sawyer, who lived in Sterling, Massachusetts. One day in 1815, Mary was on her way to school when her pet lamb followed! A statue of a lamb was erected in the town to celebrate the birthplace of Mary. There is some debate as to who actually wrote this rhyme. Some say it was written by Sarah Hale from Newport, New Hampshire, in 1830. Another theory is that Mary's classmate John Roulston wrote the poem.

# Jack and Jill

The roots of the story behind "Jack and Jill" allegedly lie in France. It is said that the two characters represent King Louis XVI (Jack), who was beheaded or "broke his crown" in 1793 during the French Revolution when the monarchy was abolished. His death was followed later that same year by his queen, Marie Antoinette (Jill), who came "tumbling after." The first publication date for the lyrics of this rhyme is 1795, which ties in with these events. "Jack and Jill" is also known as "Jack and Gill." Variant spellings in nursery rhymes are not uncommon, since they are usually passed from generation to generation by word of mouth.

# Hot Cross Buns

During Victorian times, the hot cross bun was a popular fruity snack that could be purchased from a street vendor. The Charles Dickens novel *Oliver Twist* captures the era of the street seller, and musical versions of the story feature a scene where various street sellers flood the stage brandishing their wares. Even today, hot cross buns are purchased at Easter. For Christians, the white cross on the top of the bun is an important symbol of the Easter holiday

# What Are Little Boys Made Of?

This question forms the title of a nursery rhyme that dates back to the nineteenth century. Unfortunately little boys are described as being made from unpleasant things such as snails, whereas the question "What are little girls made of?" is answered with: "Sugar and spice and all that's nice." The word *snips* may have originally read "snips of snails," meaning "small chopped-up bits of snails." There is no doubt that girls are presented in a much more favorable light in this rhyme. Would little boys enjoy the idea that they were made from things that could make girls squirm?

# Baa, Baa, Black Sheep

The wool industry was vital to Britain's economy from the Middle Ages until the nineteenth century, so it's no surprise that such a long-established trade should be celebrated in a rhyme. Some say it has a historical connection to King Edward II. The best wool in Europe was produced in England, but specialist cloth workers from the towns of Flanders, Bruges, Lille, Bergues, and Arras were better at finishing trades such as dyeing and "fulling" (cleansing, shrinking, and thickening the cloth), so the king encouraged them to improve the quality of the English wool.